MILK

MILK

A NOVEL

DARCEY STEINKE

BLOOMSBURY

Published by Bloomsbury Publishing, New York and London
Distributed to the trade by Holtzbrinck Publishers

All papers used by Bloomsbury Publishing are natural, recyclable products
made from wood grown in well-managed forests. The manufacturing
processes conform to the environmental regulations of the country of origin.

Library of Congress Cataloging-in-Publication Data

Steinke, Darcey.
Milk / Darcey Steinke.—1st U.S. ed.
p. cm.
ISBN 1-58234-529-5 (hardcover)
1. Triangles (Interpersonal relations)—Fiction. 2. Loss (Psychology)—Fiction.
3. Married women—Fiction. 4. Motherhood—Fiction. 5. Gay clergy—
Fiction. 6. Loneliness—Fiction. 7. Ex-monks—Fiction. I. Title.

PS3569.T37924M55 2005
2004012761

ISBN-13 9781582345291

First U.S. Edition 2005

1 3 5 7 9 10 8 6 4 2

Typeset by Palimpsest Book Production Limited, Polmont, Stirlingshire
Printed in the United States of America by Quebecor World Fairfield

The soul's natural inclination to love
beauty is the trap God most frequently
uses in order to win it and open it to
the breath from on high.

—Simone Weil

PART I

MARY

ONE

THE LITTLE TREE sat on a table by the window, strains of aluminum glittering and the red Christmas balls reflecting the room in concave miniature, particularly the shelf with her husband's collection of nude figurines. Mary sat on the paisley carpet, her back against the velvet couch with the frizzy fringe, and above her head a blond Keane kid in a floppy cap, eyes like sticky buns. The baby gnawed on his new teething ring; his green holiday bib was already dark around the neck with drool. Her gift from her husband's parents was raspberry-filled chocolates.

"Let's see what kind of hideousness they came up with this year," her husband said. Though Christmas was still several days away, they were opening the box from his parents in Kansas. He took a present onto his lap, shredded the Santa wrapping and passed the paper to the baby who bicycled his legs frenetically. Opening the box he lifted the tissue paper to find a Hawaiian shirt with a print of flamingoes and hibiscus flowers. Mary watched him throw down the shirt, flick his lighter and tip his head sideways toward the flame to ignite the joint. His long hair fell down in a straight line as the fire underlit the side of his face. She tried to think of something to say, but with him everything was either Good, i.e., sexy, funny, cool, or Bad, i.e., emotionally painful, boring, a hassle. You either GOT IT or you didn't GET IT. There was no reason to discuss. The baby dropped the wrapping paper and raised his tiny eyebrows when he saw the lighter's flame. He was a sucker for anything that glittered.

Inhaling, her husband held the smoke down in his lungs, his features compressed and grayed. Aided by the joint, he produced a sequence of distancing actions: widened pupils, slowing of movement, elegant tendrils of smoke. She knew he was disappointed, though every year his parents' presents were humiliating. Last year they sent a tight Speedo bathing suit and the year before the dreaded Christmas sweater. She watched him inhale again and hold the smoke down in his lungs. The radiators clanged and snow continued to rush past the window.

She took the baby onto her lap, lifted up her shirt and nursed while her husband crumpled the paper into tight little balls and loaded them into a plastic garbage bag. After a while the baby's mouth slacked off her milky nipple and he fell asleep. She laid him in his bassinet and went into the bathroom, took off her socks, jeans and sweatshirt, and stood naked as she adjusted the shower nozzle and waited for the water to warm.

On the toilet tank her husband had created an altar: a plastic bust of Darth Vader, a Jesse Ventura doll and a ceramic unicorn. Steam rolled over the top of the shower curtain. An uninterrupted shower was rare; usually she had to lay the baby on pillows on the bathroom floor and pop her head out from behind the curtain so he wouldn't cry. The inside of the porcelain tub was thoroughly spider-cracked and the shower curtain blotchy with mold. She shaved her grassy underarms and around her pubic hair. Pulling the blade along her leg, she knicked her ankle and a drop of blood fell and expanded in the water collected in the bottom of the tub. She dried herself and put on the thigh highs and teddy he'd bought her as an early Christmas present. Her stomach muscles were still loose and she had ten more pounds to lose. Her heart fluttered as she looked down at the lace against her thighs.

"Sexy girl," he said as he got up to cue another record. He was making a party tape and another techno song began, indistinguishable from the first. His face was flushed and smiling but he still moved deliberately, as if recovering from a terrible fall. She was chilly in the outfit and in the raw overhead light her skin looked powdery and loose as a latex hospital glove. It'd been since before the baby was born, and she wanted to touch him. But more than that she needed something inside. There had been a girl in high school, very tall with a long sullen face and dirty blond hair, who had the reputation for letting boys put things inside her. Fingers, real and plastic penises, candles, broom handles, turkey basters. It was rumored that once her pussy swallowed David Calloway's arm all the way up to the elbow.

After her husband changed the record, he sat on the floor by her feet. He probably didn't want to—he never did anymore—but she had to try and so leaned her head down and kissed his lips. A modicum of pressure was returned, but when she moved her tongue into his mouth, his teeth were a smooth hard line and he turned his head. She looked down at the black patch of her pubic hair beyond the lavender nylon of her panties.

"I'm beat," he said as he slipped the record back into its sleeve and turned off the lamp with the brass angels and made sure the front door was locked. He walked down the hallway and into the bedroom.

Mary sat for a while in her outfit watching tiny bits of ice stream down in the alley between their apartment building and the one next door. She watched the bits of ice rush into a cone of light, sparkle like glitter, then fall back into the dark. Already this winter forty inches of snow had fallen, and the weatherman predicted four more storm systems. She heard a guy on talk radio say it hadn't snowed as much since the winter of 1947.

Mary checked on the baby, who was sleeping on his side, one tiny foot pressed against the edge of the bassinet, and then walked into the bedroom. She lay down next to her husband, who was either sleeping, which Mary doubted, or pretending to sleep, and she, very softly, gyrated her pelvis against his ass. She felt his bones through his warm skin and her own sex tighten. But he lay still so long that she got up, changed into her flannel nightgown, went into the baby's room and lay down on the rug next to his bassinet.

When she woke much later, the room was cool and she worried that the baby wasn't warm enough. Did he need another blanket? Maybe she should have put the thicker sleeper on him. His blue eyes had looked different yesterday, slightly melancholy. Was he sick of the mobile over his crib or the song "I Left My Heart in San Francisco" that played endlessly? Too much stimulation gave babies mini–nervous breakdowns. She had read about this in an infant-care book. Also that a child's self-esteem was directly related to their mother's gaze. So it was tricky. She had to look at him enough to build self-worth but not so much he went mad. Maybe she needed to play more Mozart? Classical music made brain channels that later could be filled with algebra and calculus. If she wasn't diligent his mind would be like a block of impenetrable stone. And what about bonding? Was he attached enough to her? It was hard to tell if he was looking into her eyes or just at his own reflection. Babies in orphanages never got connected to anyone and later sometimes became serial killers. Maybe she should wake him up now and hold him; to a baby love was not abstract but visceral: warm skin, milk, her voice. Was she talking to him enough? He'd never learn to communicate if she didn't speak to him all the time. When he woke for his next feeding she would tell him the story of Watergate and the Love Canal. But those things were too dark; she'd balance them with streaking. As a little girl streaking had delighted and fascinated her. She felt the various parts of her skull, temples, sinus and her cheek-bones ache. Mary stood up; her neck was sore, as if strains of metal wire were embedded in the muscula-ture. She pressed her fingertips into the most painful spot as she walked into the other room and stood over her husband.

He snored softly, his features open and relaxed, his hair-less chest moving the silky blanket up and back. Snow brushed against the window and outside new snow coated the street, the sidewalks, the bushes, even piled delicately up on tree branches. The traffic light changed from green to red.

Tonight, snow muffled the car tires and ticked like sugar granules on the window ledge. Snow created a silence similar to the silence of God. God was where your mind went when it wasn't thinking of anything in particular. She stared at the paisley carpet. Pine needles from the Christmas tree floated in the weave. She watched the carpet; red light from the tree bewitched the wool threads. Mary pulled up her nightgown, the one with the blood-stain on the back from her first days home from the hospital, pulled it up gently around her thighs like a girl wading into a river.

After his three A.M. feeding the baby wouldn't sleep; he was fussy and agitated, so she told him the plot of *Anna Karenina*, leaving out all the boring agrarian details, and explained that in "The Beast in the Jungle," Marcher was definitely gay. She told the story of the turtle and the hare and tried the fox and the grapes, though once she established the fox sitting there watching the bunch of grapes she couldn't remember exactly what had happened.

The key was to keep talking so the baby would be soothed by her voice and fall asleep. She felt his little fist against her collarbone and his tiny kneecap pressed into her breast, and wondered why he was so upset. She began to tell him the Christmas story, starting with the angel coming to Mary, ran through the star, the Wise Men, the divine baby sleeping in straw. Then to Jesus' later childhood when he was left in the temple but she couldn't remember the order of his miracles, and after the fishes and the loaves she got discouraged and started telling him what all the various religions thought happened to you after you died, how Jews didn't believe in heaven or hell and how the Hindus believed in reincarnation. She could come back as a lamb; he could come back as a butterfly. The resurrection sounded ludicrous so she covered its grim details quickly.

Snowflakes big as quarters slapped wetly against the glass, and the baby's heart was like a tiny fluttery bird pinned inside his chest. She was so tired she was near tears and she missed her own mother's generous lap and her way with a hamburger, and while she knew her mother was now with God, she was confused about where certain aspects of her personality had gone. Her interest in the occult and the British royal family, the way she laughed even at the smallest joke like it was hysterical. The baby started to scream. What else? She'd exhausted all of her oral information and now felt shapeless as a larva. Maybe it was colic. His arms flung around, and he twisted his head against the collar of her nightgown.

Mary walked into the kitchen to switch on the faucet and let the water mesmerize him. But there was no need, as sparks were falling from the ceiling. At first she thought someone was welding in the apartment above. But who did ironwork at this hour? Besides, the sparks weren't falling but hovering like fireflies. Maybe there was an electrical short inside the wall. Either way the baby was distracted, he hung onto her neck with his little hands and stared up at the bobbing flames, his mouth wide open.

With one hand she swung the broom up, tried to knock out the tiny fires, but strains of straw just went through the mass as though it were a hologram. A reflection, Mary thought, remembering how once on a train she'd seen what looked like a small pond suspended over a field; it had undulated like tinfoil before the train turned. She glanced out the window into the narrow alley; no moon, and clouds covered the stars. Not enough light really for a reflected magic trick. The lights churned with the same motion as glitter inside a snow dome. The motion enchanted the baby, who bicycled his legs again and rocked his whole body forward.

Two

WALTER HAD FESTOONED St. Paul's front doors with evergreen garlands and the little statue of the Holy Mother wore a holly wreath around her head. Mary opened the iron side gate; the metal was cold on her fingers and she walked the icy path. Inside, the walls along the corridor were missing chunks of plaster, and Walter's door was open, his office filled with smoke. He was addicted to incense, the rare variety produced by the Benedictine monks of Prinknash; sometimes his room was as smoky as a rock concert.

"Mary," he said, looking up from his laptop; the screen's blue light underlit his face and highlighted his black curly hair. He could be working on his Christmas sermon, but he also frequented a chat room for theologically minded adherents of S&M. The computer light was the room's only illumination. His bookshelf, the paintings of St. Paul's former ministers, and all the other ministerial objects were cloaked in a vaporous gloom. Walter pulled the little chain on his desk lamp and the Jesus shade lit up, incense swirling above.

"Thanks for letting me come. I know it's busy, with Christmas and everything," Mary said while laying her coat over the warm radiator and unzipping the baby's snowsuit. Static from his polar-fleece cap made his hair stand on end.

"Look at the little punk rocker." Walter laughed. "Can I hold him?"

"If you take off that smoky sweater." Mary glanced at the cigarette butts in the glass ashtray. "What happened to the patch?"

"It didn't work; it was like getting the Holy Spirit when you want Jesus." Walter took the baby onto his lap and kissed the top of his head. There was a tap on the door and Junot, the teenage custodian, stepped into the room. His jeans rode so low on his hips Mary could see Mickey Mouse on his boxers. He was a good-looking kid with olive skin and coffee-colored eyes.

"What needs to be done today, Father?" he asked.

Walter had given up explaining that he was an Episcopal, not a Catholic, priest.

"I have a list here," he said, passing over a piece of loose-leaf paper. "And I guess you better bring up the crèche. I think it's tacky, but the Sunday school director wants it out there."

Junot nodded and retreated down the hallway.

"So do you think I'm crazy?" Mary asked.

Walter looked into her eyes, then glanced at her fingers worrying a Kleenex. She knew he was thinking of last summer when a voice had told her to fill the bathtub with dirt and plant flowers. Or that time in college when she'd been determined a little Yorkie had said her name.

Junot walked past the doorway carrying a plastic camel, the electrical cord wrapped around the animal's long golden leg. The baby whined and Walter jostled him on his knee.

"Well. So. You have this baby," he began, "this little creature that came through you but from the Great Beyond, or maybe I should say the Great Before or in any case another plane." He paused; it was when he gave spiritual advice that Walter most resembled the stoner he'd been in college. "So that's disturbing, right?"

Mary nodded. Junot walked past the doorway again, this time carrying plastic sheep, one under each arm. The glass paperweight on Walter's desk transfixed the baby. Mary knew he thought it was edible.

"So maybe you feel curious about this spiritual plane and you feel you want some contact with it . . ."

Mary nodded. She heard Junot coming down the hallway.

"I mean you probably think God resides out somewhere in the universe, right? So in your mind you need a conduit."

She did feel a need for some sort of portal. "I guess that's right, though you make it sound like a *Star Trek* episode."

Junot, who had overheard what Walter was saying, stuck his head into the doorway. He held a shepherd in a cream-colored robe. "Father, do you think if you step on a crack your soul flies out from your body?"

"Who told you that?"

"My mother," Junot said. "It happened to her." Junot lived with his mother in the Smith Street projects. She was, according to him, in nearly constant contact with the spirit world. She spoke to God in the middle of breakfast, condemning him for her lousy night's sleep. She prayed on the subway, in the grocery store. When her sister in Puerto Rico was sick, Junot said her prayers were like a form of surveillance.

"Did she get it back?" Mary asked.

"Oh, she has some story about an angel putting her soul back. This was after she'd been through three trials. She had to assist a stranger in need. Help a sick animal. I think she fed a stray cat for that one."

"And the last one?" Walter asked.

"She had to speak with a flower."

"She talked to it?" Mary said.

"Yeah, that's how she knew which night the angel would come."

"And you believe all this?" Walter asked.

Junot shrugged and smiled. "I guess," he said as he walked back down the hall toward the church basement.

The baby's eyes bulged a little and he spit up a few drops of curdled milk.

"Oh dear," Walter said, passing him back to Mary and using a Kleenex to wipe off his black pants.

She heard pounding footsteps on the basement stairs, and Junot ran into the office. He was holding the baby Jesus. The plastic baby was no bigger then a football. His legs, arms and head were peach. He had blue eyes, blond hair and wore a tiny white toga. Junot held Jesus up to Walter's face. "FUCK YOU" was written on the infant's forehead in black Magic Marker.

On the subway ride back home Mary tried to pray. *Lord Jesus, have mercy on me*, but her words were overwhelmed with the Desitin Ointment she needed to buy for the baby's rash, the ear thermometer, that weird thing her husband had said about the French actress's ass. Over her head was a placard poem about how numbers repeated rapaciously into infinity, how apples never lie, how the body at best is a transitory vehicle. A few seats down, a pale man wearing an aviator's cap began to cough, his hack like syrup at rapid boil.

The baby fell asleep, his body warm as a patch of sunlight against her sweater, his tiny mouth open and his eyelids as fragile as flower petals. Maybe he dreamt of the time before his conception when he'd inhabited every blade of grass. She figured he could read the consciousness of objects; that's why the pot of ivy fascinated him, as if each shiny leaf transmuted an idea. He got as much from watching the aura around a lightbulb as the expression on her face. He slept, drooling into the material of the baby carrier, until the thud of the elevator doors jolted him awake.

As she unlocked the front door of her apartment, he arched his back, wrinkled his face up and screamed. Mary pulled off her coat, unbuttoned her blouse and yanked down the flap of her nursing bra. At the scent of her body, the baby agitated his face against her nipple like a baby bird. His tiny features relaxed as he latched on and sucked. The glands high in her breast tingled as her milk came down. Usually her milk was exclusively for the baby, but occasionally the sweet liquid came for flood victims on television and when the homeless man asked her for a quarter. Sometimes she leaked milk when the neighbor's dog barked or at the memory of how excited her mother got during her favorite TV show. The baby emptied her breast, and so she shifted him, hand cupped around his black hair, and forced his mouth onto her left.

At first she'd read magazines while nursing: articles about endangered albino owls, and how a deaf doctor was the best surgeon in Soviet Russia. But now any word longer than two syllables exhausted her and made her feel nervous. So she stared out the window at the snow coming down, until the baby's mouth released her nipple and she burped him against her shoulder, changed his wet diaper and lay him in his bassinet.

She tiptoed out of the room and flung herself down on her bed, listening to the sound of the occasional car tires muted and lovely in the new snow. No matter how tired her muscles felt or how much her head ached, blood raced in her veins. She tried again to pray. *Come, Lord Jesus, have mercy on me.* But the mole above her left eyebrow started to throb. Was it cancerous? She jumped up to check it in the bathroom mirror. Settling down again, she imagined sweeping all her petty thoughts off the end of a dock with a long bristly janitor's broom, but just when her head felt clear, she thought about the steak and mashed potatoes she wanted to make for dinner, that she needed dental floss and more liquid Tylenol.

The sensation of the baby's lips on her nipple lingered. Walter would understand; he himself believed in the necessity of physical pleasure. So she dragged her pointer finger over her tongue and slid her hand beneath the waistband of her underpants. She felt her clit begin to rotate. Only God could infuse something so rudimentary with life. She was made out of cosmic refuse—stardust, smoky vapor—and so occasionally if she concentrated, she could tease down the life force for her own selfish use.

She sank her finger inside herself, and really, though she didn't mean to brag, she was ridiculously wet and decided therefore to split the universe. *Fuck me*, she said, and then again, but more politely, *Fuck me, please.* There was so much vulgarness inside her; it was beautiful really. But she could be tender too. She planned to ask the Man at the coffee shop about the scar over his right eyebrow and he would tell her that as a little boy he'd fallen onto the ice. And that worked for a while: the little boy falling onto the cold, hard ice, wet blood pooling above his blue eye, a drop or two saturating the snow.

The phone sounded like the twill of a metal bird. Her husband calling from the office to tell her HE wanted to come home but that THEY wanted him to go out to another Christmas party. The baby shifted in the bassinet, and Mary closed her eyes and went directly to the babysitter's thin teenage body entwined with her boyfriend's thin teenage body, as they fucked crazily on the couch. And for a while that was okay, the scent of Coca-Cola and sweat as their flat stomachs and sharp hips collided. But then it wasn't enough and it was time for the father to walk over to the couch, lower his pants and offer the babysitter his cock.

This worked immediately; a sweet sting infused her flesh. But just as quickly the water began to leak out of the drain. And she tried frantically to inhabit each of them, father, babysitter, boyfriend. Each had characteristics as mysterious as the holy trinity. She decided to kick the babysitter out. But it was too late. She was the babysitter, the unbabysitter, the ur-babysitter, the ghost in the babysitter. She tensed her pelvis and a swarm of butterflies careened up her spine. The vibrations entered her like radio waves, her bones felt molten and she was a twig pitched out into the universe. And that WAS IT: Her sex twitched and she felt the lobes of her brain open like a flower and she was inside of a wave, made from torn-up flower petals. Broken petals filling her mouth as she swung open the car door and staggered away from the crash. Flames jumping from the engine, her head banged up and spacey, her pelvis tipped and aching as if she actually had gotten fucked. Blood beat inside her ear and as the impact dissipated, her sadness swelled. Nothing had changed. Sure, the snow under the car tires had degenerated into slush, but that had more to do with decay than divinity and it was infuriating, really, having to wait so long for him to come.

THREE

WHEN MARY WOKE at two A.M. her husband was still not home. The baby slept pressed against her breast like a puppy in a litter, and she was afraid if she slept again she'd smother him with her hair. She heard this had happened in Utah, a baby choked by sucking a clump of his mother's hair; she heard too that a father had forgotten his baby in a car seat and that the baby, in the heat of the sealed car, had died. She heard that a helicopter blade had decapitated a baby, and that a grandmother on a ferryboat had lost her grip and her tiny granddaughter had disappeared into the boat's churning water.

The baby whimpered and agitated his mouth. She carried him to the front room, sat on the blue chair and helped him latch on to her nipple. Objects in the dark glinted, as if mica chips ran through everything. Her lucidity was terrifying; she wanted her consciousness to break down into softer parts. So she ran through all the car games she'd played as a kid. Telling the baby how first she would ask a silly question and then her mother would ask an even sillier one: *Can I eat my hat for lunch? Are your underpants made of ice cream? Did you like your butterfly sandwich?* And then the other game where her mother would give her a choice between two things: *Would you rather be a dog or a cat? Would you rather be a cheese sandwich or a toasted cheese sandwich?*

The phone started its electronic purr and for some reason she thought of an image from her childhood: President Kennedy's wounded head, not scary now, just soft and sad. After the beep her husband said, *These jokers are keeping me out all night.* Muffled shouts, a girl said something in French and then her husband again: *If I can get a cab, I'll be home soon, if not, I'll have to take the subway.* And it was in the silence after the tape rolled back as she set the baby in his bassinet that a flash of light came from a source behind her. She turned and saw the sparks hovering again but this time in the corner of the bedroom.

She walked closer; each diorama showed a different

scene. A porcelain lamp, a fluorescent panel, each smaller than a pea but so particular, as if her eyes were as powerful as microscopes. A chrome lamp showed a woman cutting the fingernails of a small child, and an oak tree was silhouetted by a streetlight. She stepped closer and saw the expression on the face of an old man reading a newspaper.

Outside half-hearted flurries swirled down over the sidewalk. She'd decided to put the baby into the carrier and walk down to the Brooklyn Bridge.

Flakes collected on the shoulders of her coat, and the cold bit into her bare hands. Since the very first week of her pregnancy all her senses had been elevated. She was like a wolf, able to smell cigarette smoke from half a block away and warm Chinese food from the restaurant on Court Street. Her vision was sharper too; she could make out every nuance of the rotting leaves between the grates of the gutter. Static snow flew around, and it was so quiet she could hear her own footfalls and so looked down at her boots making patterns in the fine layer of sidewalk snow.

She looked up to the lower Manhattan skyline. Office windows lit up like links in a gold chain. Flakes whirled around as she stood on the cobblestones between

Bargemusic and the River Café. Bee lights covered the maples. Above them, the stone base of the bridge, steel girders fanning out. Through the restaurant's sliding doors she saw a bartender in a white jacket move into view, pick up a glass and step toward the liquor bottles, which were tiny and radiant as jewels.

When she got home her husband was sleeping fully clothed on the bed, his hair reeking of cigarette smoke. She watched him for a while, his chest moving up and down, his eyelids jerking in REM sleep. He was very beautiful with his long face and narrow shoulders, like a stone prince on top of a crypt. When she first met him her own father had just gotten married again and she'd been new to New York City and lonely. He was a bike messenger with a long ponytail, he smoked joints in the back of churches on his rounds and on the weekends took her to raves where they took ecstasy and danced in crowds of sweaty people. Stellar sex always followed and she wanted him past all of her experience of wanting. Wanting him was like wanting the moon, an aloof and glamorous disk of shifting light.

The baby began to whine. She changed his diaper, then sat with him in the blue chair, but each time she offered her nipple, he pursed his lips and turned his face away. To calm him she walked around the apartment. It was as ritualistic as the Stations of the Cross, beginning with her polka-dot shirt; she held up the shirt on its hanger and he grew pensive. Before the pattern ceased to interest him, she moved on to the ivy plant, that one particular leaf that fascinated him, and she felt him relax his weight against her shoulder; his head fell into the crook of her neck and he slept.

FOUR

M ARY ORDERED MINT tea and a cranberry muffin and sat in a chair in back listening to Christmas jazz and watching snow blow horizontally past the front window. The wood tables were mostly empty, just a young woman in a ponytail writing out Christmas cards and the Man at his usual table in back. She glanced at him as he wrote in his notebook. Sometimes he used a felt-tip marker and other times she saw him use a pencil to trace a blueprint, a long sprawling single-story house. He always wore the same outfit: khaki pants creased down the front and a white button-down shirt, each cuff folded back neatly to the elbow. His shoulders were heavy and wider than her husband's, and he had wrinkles around his eyes.

She sat down. The baby's face was smushed against the side of the carrier, and he was elfin in his little green cap and matching mittens. He grimaced in his sleep. She shouldn't have had that slice of onion on her tuna fish at lunch. Onions did odd things to her milk. She rocked forward to comfort him. Snowflakes outside zigzagged across the window, and inside, the wood grain of her table glimmered. She watched the counter girl use silver tongs to lay glazed donuts out in the display case.

Her husband's story about last night was rickety, particularly his account of the hours between two and when he reached home at five. Instead of being contrite, he was angry about her questions. She'd ruined everything by being jealous; now he didn't want to stay home Christmas Eve. They'd planned to make dinner and watch a video, open the presents she had bought for the baby. Now he was going to the Orphan's Party his friend Roger threw every year.

Mary yelped and sprang up; something had bitten her leg. A hand laid down a wedge of napkins over the spilled tea, and when she turned she saw the Man leaning forward, so close she could have touched his face.

"Sorry," Mary said, motioning to the tipped paper teacup. "I'm clumsy."

"Not to worry," he said. "Are you wet?"

Mary examined the baby and then her coat for spots, but the tea had only stained her pant leg. "I'm fine," she said.

The Man hesitated; he didn't seem to want to go back to his own table. "You look tired."

Mary blushed. "I guess I am," she said. "You know, not a lot, just a little." She pressed her fingernails into the palm of her hand and thought of herself in her ratty coat moving around the neighborhood.

"My name is John." He held out his hand.

"Mary," she said, touching his thick fingers.

"Can I sit here?" he said, pulling out a chair.

Mary looked at the empty chair and nodded.

"What are you reading?" She pointed to the book splayed in half on the table.

"Poincaré this evening. I'm rather taken with his claim that he could move material objects from one closed container to another."

"Could he?" Mary asked.

"Probably not. He also insisted that once when he rotated a cup"—he swirled his coffee—"a little sparrow flew out of the bottom."

Mary saw in his blue eyes a few specks of white which shifted slowly like plastic chips in a snow dome.

"Did he have any theories about air having the same properties as paper?"

John's expression didn't change but his eyebrows shifted up. "How do you mean?"

"It's going to sound crazy," Mary said, "but reality can get these little pinprick holes."

John leaned forward conspiratorially; the tea bag in his paper cup looked like a blouted trout. "What you describe sounds like an aleph, a point in space that contains all points. The most famous one on record was in 1938. A boy living with his mother in an apartment in Barcelona claimed he saw the night sky swarming with tiny lights whenever he rolled up his mother's bread bin."

"Just the one scene?"

"My guess is that the poor boy confused what he was seeing—the entire world from every angle simultaneously— with a meteor shower. You can understand his mistake, all those light sources swirling at once."

"So other people have seen it?"

John nodded and blushed from the rim of his hairline all the way out to his earlobes, and Mary saw that the scar over his eyebrow was shaped more like a raisin than a sunflower seed. She looked over to his notebook where he had drawn a star configuration. "Canis Major" was written out at the top and there were little arrows pointing to Sirius and Aludra.

The baby slept sprawled out on John's futon as he carried the bottle of brandy over to the table. He was not as handsome as her husband. John's face was plain, but there was something behind it, not light exactly, though light's focused beam was part of her understanding of his appeal. As she laid out the details of her life—baby, husband, how she wanted to write poetry but had become a schoolteacher instead—she took in the décor of his apartment, the futon, chest of drawers, marble fireplace. No television or radio, just a dozen books on the window ledge. Hanging over the mantel was a crucifix; a wasted wooden Jesus on a metal cross.

"That's the only thing I brought from my cell."

Mary felt her jaw drop and her mouth fall open. His thick upper arms, his crew cut; she glanced at his hands for jailbird tattoos.

John laughed. "No. No. No. It's not what you think. I use to live in a monastery."

"With the monks?"

He set two teacups on the table and tipped the brandy bottle into each. "I was a monk."

Mary saw him in a long robe walking along a stone corridor. "What happened?"

He sat back in his chair. "It's a good question. I think if my dissatisfaction had been parceled out, things might have been different. But one day during the long silence in the middle of diurnum, I just realized that after fifteen years I was no closer to God than the day I entered." He looked out onto the dark street.

The baby began to cry, and Mary picked him up and pressed him against her shoulder. "I'm afraid he's hungry," she said. "I need to get back."

"You can nurse him. I don't mind," John said.

Mary looked at him tentatively, but the baby was animated, agitating his head like a baby bird and crying so hard his face was red and his whole body trembled. She took the cloth diaper out of her pocket and laid it over her shoulder, unbuttoned her shirt and reached under to unlatch the flap of her nursing bra. Her face got hot as he slurped, and she stared down at the baby's tiny elbows, his hands under the cloth cupping her breast.

John held his body at an awkward angle, as if she wasn't nursing but amputating somebody's leg.

"I can stop," she said.

"No!" he said fiercely, his expression drawn, his eyes flooding with water.

FIVE

THE ORPHANS' CHRISTMAS Party was in the East Village. Chili-pepper lights encircled the windows and the refrigerator was filled with beer. All the furniture was pushed back to the wall and there were sagging bodega roses around in coffee cups. About a dozen people had already arrived, all younger than her, and mostly women who worked at the production company with her husband. Her husband got her a glass of seltzer, and they leaned on the window casement and talked about the baby.

He liked the goofy expression the baby made when he was angry and how much he loved that one leaf on the ivy plant in the living room. How he'd suck on anything, a dirty T-shirt, the side of a cereal box. As he talked, his eyes followed a young woman in leather pants around the party. *You've been so freaked out lately. I wish you could be mellower.* She could tell by the way he moved his hand around that he was getting drunk. *The God stuff, you know that's a bunch of bullshit.*

A guy that her husband used to know came up and he talked about how happy he was not to be at his mother's condo in Florida. He wore a porkpie hat and a Kraftwerk T-shirt. *It was so depressing down there with all the old people.* A tall girl joined them, introducing herself as China. *Thank the Lord, I don't have to go to Memphis. My father is so Republican and my mother is a Zoloft zombie.* Mary's husband smiled widely. Mary looked around at people gathering on the couches and chairs. Most had dressed up; a girl wore silver eyelashes, and one of the guys had on a tuxedo jacket. The Christmas tree was decorated with matchbooks, and below the tree the ceramic crèche was painted with garish colors. The Wise Men were kitsch of the highest order, situated between a lawn flamingo and a ceramic bust of Elvis.

The girl in the leather pants came out of the kitchen carrying a drink and her husband began again to follow her with his eyes. Mary felt her ears ringing and, though she didn't have to, she said she had to pee.

Inside the bathroom, the porcelain was white as bone and the shower curtain covered with tiny black skulls. Someone had left a half-cup of eggnog on the sink and she remembered that it was the night people wait for the birth of the überbaby. Her own labor was stitched into her mind. The pain made her penetrable—air, light, noise; all these moved through her. Blood, mixed with amniotic fluid and scented like seaweed, had run down her legs as she bore down and felt her pelvis opening, her consciousness as if made from paper, ripping in two. Somebody knocked on the door; she flushed the toilet for effect and ran the faucet.

When she got back her husband was talking to a girl with a choker, whom he introduced as Sonya. The music was louder now, so Mary had to yell to be heard. Sonya said her mom was in Saint Bart's with her boyfriend and her father was with his third wife up in Westchester. She rolled her eyes and pointed out that the expression on the Virgin Mary's face was like a porn star's. Mary's husband stared at the band of black leather around Sonya's neck and her small well-delineated breasts under her tight T-shirt.

It's so weird you have a baby, she kept saying. Mary felt

her breasts swell with milk. *I mean, I could never handle a baby. A baby. God, that would totally freak me out.*

The lamp was on in John's apartment. An orb of light fell over his table, but he wasn't sitting in his chair and he wasn't sleeping on his futon either. Cold bit into the tips of her hands, and she took her fingers off the iron fence and sunk them into her pockets. Tinsel was woven into the snow sloped against the brownstone, and there was a wreath, with a red ribbon, on his door.

"Are you waiting for me?"

She spun around, and there he was with a swing bag of groceries hanging from his right hand. His head was bare and a puff of steam dispersed before his lips.

"I can only stay a minute," she said, waiting for him to unlock his front door. Inside he nodded to the chairs by the table and went into the kitchen. Mary heard the sound of crinkling plastic as he put away the groceries. He'd bought himself a few things for Christmas, a pumpkin pie and a rotisserie chicken. She laid her coat on the bed and sat at the wood table; she read the word "aniseikonia" in his journal and the definition—"when one eye sees an object as bigger than the other."

"You look nice," he said as he carried in the teacups and the bottle of brandy.

"I was out at a party," she said. She watched him settle into his chair and lay down a stack of napkins.

He was wearing a blue sweater with holes at the elbows and his face carried a flush of cold. He looked at her intently.

"I'm sorry about yesterday."

"It makes a lot of people uncomfortable," Mary said.

"It's not that," he said, walking over to the mantel and picking up a snapshot. He handed her the photo. "You see," he said, "I almost had a family."

The photo was faded, curled at the edges. A woman in a calico dress smiled at the camera. She wore feather earrings and her stomach was huge. "It happened twenty-four years ago. I got the call right around dinnertime. My wife had pulled off the highway to help a lady with a flat tire. But it was foggy and a truck hit her while she walked along the shoulder."

"I'm sorry," Mary said as she stared at the photo. The woman held one hand under her stomach and one hand on top, displaying her pregnant belly. Her pale hair hung around her face, and her lips were open as if she were about to speak. Mary handed the photo back and he slipped it inside the pages of his notebook. He sat very still and stared down at the gold liquid in his cup.

Mary moved her hand across the wood and touched his fingers, and he leaned forward and kissed her mouth. His lips were not food exactly, but just as sustaining, and she opened her mouth and his tongue came inside all delicate flickers and so much more lively and nuanced than she would have anticipated.

Everything was going pretty well except that she felt bad about his dead wife and baby. Felt bad for crack addicts, bad about the Middle East, bad that people got operations they didn't need because of the American medical machine. But then she opened her eyes and every object seemed as delicately constructed as the baby's loose tummy. Everything had soft bones configured into beautiful skeletal patterns; she was just a fragment of the world seeking another fragment. He came around to Mary's side of the table and turned off the lamp and picked her up and carried her to his futon.

Light from the window made a little shadow-puppet theater of snow coming down on the wall above them. He said into her hair, *It's been a really long time.* And she tugged at his belt and helped him pull down his pants; boxers over skinny white legs. She yanked off her tights and lay back in her bra. Her nursing bra, which was wide and puffy. She wasn't sure if she wanted to take it off. Her breasts might leak.

A couple walked by on the street talking. She remembered the baby; her breasts were so tight she knew he'd need to nurse soon. But John was kissing her neck, all down the raised tendons and on the soft skin between, and she began to feel his cock defining itself, like a little god, against her thigh. Hadn't she been a good person? Hadn't she sold Girl Scout cookies and collected every Halloween for UNICEF? Didn't she recycle? she thought as she moved between his legs and set her tongue against that delicate circumcised V. Tasting the first bit of cum, musty, green, she closed her mouth and sucked as if his cock were a tiny breast, and she slid her tongue inside the slit at the tip and tasted salt; and there began the slow descent into the animal kingdom where the halos around streetlights seemed to be singing, and she remembered how, when the baby's head first appeared between her legs, she'd felt for a moment like a circus freak.

She put her hand between his thighs, traced her fingers

over his balls, then reached into the crack of his ass and pressed her pointer finger against his anus and she wanted butterflies to gather in a heap on her abdomen and the ice teaspoon to spill its dirt. She needed soil for the garden and the rose trestle and the little lamb who recited French poetry. He pulled her up to his face, and Mary rocked her pelvis against his and looked up at the tiny black shadows falling down over the wall and over his features; his face was wet. Water trickled out the edge of his eyes. Mary rolled on top of him, and they kissed until his cock dug into her stomach. She reached back and unlatched her bra; her breasts fell forward, heavy as water balloons. The sensation made his eyes jump open and he strained his head up, took her nipple into his mouth. His brow furrowed and his features compressed with intense pleasure at the taste of her milk.

When she finally got home her husband still wasn't there, and she paid the sitter and walked to where the baby slept. He'd kicked the blanket off and she pulled it up to his chin. She turned the Christmas tree lights on in the front room and sat down in the blue chair. The lights illuminated the pine needles and tinsel. She saw the silver church with the snow on the roof and the miniature present wrapped in green paper and the painted rocking horse and the crocheted snowflakes and the little silver bell; and she watched snow fall into the dark alley and brush against the window.

Walter always said that the chief thing that separates us from God is the thought that we are separate from him. But really, at the moment, that sounded to her like a bunch of bullshit. She walked down the hall and swung open the closet door. On the floor was a box filled with shoes, her mother's house slippers mixed with sneakers and vinyl thrift-store boots. The mop lay in the bucket beside a lampshade and a bag of old videos.

She kneeled down. The sleeve of her ratty wool coat brushed her forehead. Inside her coat pocket was a half-sucked cough drop. Inside the cough drop were atoms, and she knew that atoms, like flowers, had individual parts, protons and neurons. Mary pressed her palms against each other and squeezed her eyes shut. The world was on the edge of revolution, pregnant with a different kind of life.

PART II

WALTER

ONE

THROUGH THE DOORWAY of his office, Walter watched Mary help Junot paint the hall. The trustees had agreed she could stay in the rectory rent-free as long as she helped with the church's renovations. Mary painted the baseboard with a brush, while Junot, using a roller, got at the wall higher up. She was on her hands and knees and Walter could see the dark roots of her hair and how tendons stood out from her neck.

It'd been a month since she'd left her husband. Christmas had transpired as had New Year's, and while her crying jags diminished, she still felt flimsy. Her features were not unified, but seemed at odds with one another. Shades of pink, yellow and a delicate blue showed through in her complexion.

The baby lay in a basket beside his desk; the former laundry hamper now tricked out like the reed-boat that had carried Moses. He coughed as he held an athletic sock in a tiny fisted hand. Mary insisted the baby had allergies but he worried; the cough sounded harsh and adult. Walter grasped the end of the sock and jiggled; the baby smiled and bicycled his legs. He felt responsible for Mary; if he were straight they'd be married and the baby would be his own. He loved how the baby sometimes held his hands out when he wanted to be picked up and how the rectory now smelled like melted butter. In the evening when Mary nursed the baby by the fire, the white skin of her breast marbled with blue veins, her face flushed with exhaustion and the baby's face was as new and uncorrupted as a peach.

He glanced back down at the bills, slips of perforated paper, spread out next to the computer. The gas was the most substantial; even with the thermometer at sixty the cavernous church was ridiculously expensive to heat. Walter's calculator was beside him. All told, St. Paul's expenses were twice as much as the amount in the checking account. Walter thought of calling Mrs. Newberry, though he'd just made his New Year's visit. He'd been as explicit as possible, given the form of the pastoral house call, but she had not written him a check. Silk was the only answer, and he dialed the bishop's private number at the cathedral and left a message about getting together for lunch.

Walter heard Junot's roller in the tray and then paint spreading over the wall; the delicate sound was akin to snow falling but wetter and less ethereal. He glanced over to his computer screen; the picture of a man in a brown fedora still hovered. Walter couldn't decide about his face, though he did like that he'd named his dog Elmo. And he wasn't too faggy; those guys obsessed with ABBA and Liza Minnelli made his skin crawl. Under favorite book was listed Barbara Kingsolver, *Poisonwood Bible*. Ugh. But not everybody was into Meister Eckehart and Julian of Norwich. What the hey. The man had nice ears, like shells, the lobes oversized and artistic-looking.

"Mary?" Walter said, as he swung open the closet door. He'd seen what looked like her black boots and then realized her legs and knees where attached. "What are you doing in there?"

Her face poked through the sleeves of coats dangling from wooden hangers, and she stood up between brown boxes of Carlos memorabilia, her head floating as if in water above the blue and gray collars of the woolen coats.

"Praying," she said. "Closets are like little chapels, don't you think?" Her expression was sheepish. Earlier that day she had asked if he thought there was any connection between astrology and Christianity, and what did it mean that Jesus was a Capricorn?

Her face seemed narrower than usual; there were burgundy circles under her eyes and sweat on her upper lip. Walter had seen her like this before, like last summer when a voice had instructed her to fill her bathtub with dirt and plant flowers. The time before she'd gotten fascinated with the mailbox at the corner of Cranberry and Henry. But the worst was in college when, in a dream, God had urged her to save the world through prayer. Mary had rushed into his dorm in the middle of the night with this news, her pupils dilated and her voice solemn with stewardship. She'd told him that all the furry animals being born in the woods around their university were divine, that they'd bring into existence a common language, one that the entire world would understand, people as well as dolphins and butterflies. When he'd suggested she take one of his Valiums, she'd been offended and locked herself in her dorm room, praying for seventy-two consecutive hours until, exhausted, her sweatpants damp with urine, she'd fallen asleep.

"Did you take your Saint-John's-wort today?"

Mary nodded. "When I'm sad, sometimes I go into my closet and lay on my shoes."

A part of him wanted to insist again that she wean the baby and get on Zoloft. He wanted her to act normal, to behave in a conventional manner so he could worry less. But what difference did it make really if you prayed by the side of your bed or underneath it?

"My dog did that during thunderstorms." He saw his umbrella, a thrift-store model with a handle shaped like a tree branch. "Will you pass me that?"

She complied.

"Don't wait up," he said, and there was an awkward pause. "You can carry on if you'd like."

"Okay," she said, her head disappearing again between the jackets.

"Do you want me to shut the door?"

"If you wouldn't mind," she said, her voice muffled by the wool and cashmere coats.

* * *

The man from Match.com had a sandpapery voice and a rapid delivery that mesmerized Walter. His hair had grown since the photo into a strawberry-blond mop; strands fell over his eyes as he gesticulated. He'd been raised on the Upper West Side. His mother was German and his father the editor of a cooking magazine. He pronounced his name Sta-fon. He was an actor, mostly TV commercials. He'd been the fire ant in the Ortho spot and the voice of a character called Tiny Duck Man in a popular Saturday-morning kids' cartoon.

Walter watched him as he moved his hands, relating the story of his first sexual experience—always a mainstay of these encounters, or the good ones anyway, the ones where a pretense of connection had to be established before sex. Walter was pleased that he found Sta-fon engaging; he was trying to be good. He'd always been attracted to teenagers, but after Carlos died they had an almost magnetic pull. Particularly that boy at Heavenly Rest. Nothing physical had happened, but when the boy's mother found The Love Letter she went ballistic, complained to Bishop Silk and forced his resignation from the Upper East Side church. Silk threatened to send him overseas to do missionary work but in the end he'd arranged with his friend the bishop of Long Island for the job in Brooklyn.

He listened to Sta-fon's story intently, as he moved through the attributes of the lecherous drama coach, a familiar archetype in any gay adolescence, interchangeable with the lecherous basketball coach or the lecherous priest. The dramatist wooed with emerald cuff links and a collection of Picasso prints. At the end of the semester, he'd invited Sta-fon over for a private performance of *Krapp's Last Tape* and a bottle of scotch. Walter could tell he had told the story before but not how many times. His eyes kept changing from sea green to lavender.

Walter's own seduction story was grim, its main components being a kitchen table and an evil stepfather, and so he always lied. There were several versions he relied on; the lifeguard at camp was the most popular. But today he decided to go free form, explaining how his mother's family owned the largest ranch in Montana. This fantasy mother, he explained, had taught him to rope and ride as well as make a venison chili that the Quilted Giraffe would be lucky to serve. A half-dozen cowboys ran the place, and when he was thirteen, a couple of them agreed to take him up-country on an overnight.

"There was an individual," Walter said—he could tell Sta-fon believed him by the way he leaned forward, his

sweater almost brushing the foam of his second latte—
"a half-Mexican fellow known as Juan. He ate M&M's
and was always singing Led Zeppelin songs."

"Jesus," Sta-fon said, "it's like a movie."

"Yeah, it was," Walter said. "So anyway in the middle
of the night I got up to go to the bathroom and on my
way back I saw Juan walking toward me. And that was,
as they say, a fait accompli."

"Wow," Sta-fon said, and he adjusted himself in his
chair, a pained expression infiltrating his features. He had
a potbelly, and Walter assumed all the talk of hard-chested
cowboys had made him self-conscious.

"Do you ever make stuff up just for the heck of it?"
Sta-fon said as he looked past Walter's head to the snowy
street. Hairs on the back of his neck stood up and he had
the sensation that he was cornered, each shoulder blade
touching a wall. A thump of blood moved from his heart
out into his veins. No one had ever questioned his seduction story before. Maybe he should have stuck to the
standards like the Little League coach or the heterosexual
one that featured a best friend's mother. He was confused.
These Match.com encounters were typically friendly; men
who dated online rarely wanted to see you more than once.

"It's all true," Walter said, "right down to his straw cowboy hat."

Sta-fon stared into his coffee cup and there was an awkward silence as Walter watched the waitress with the ponytail carrying a cappuccino topped with whipped cream and sprinkled with cocoa to a table nearby.

"You seem like a nice person," Sta-fon said. "Do you want to tell me what actually happened?"

Walter felt his face get hot; the way Sta-fon spoke reminded Walter of a schoolteacher instructing children, and his face, while open and friendly, seemed premeditatedly so. Probably a twelve-stepper, Walter thought; soon he'll begin his drunk-a-log and start reciting all those platitudes. *One day at a time. Fake it till you make it. Easy does it. Do the next right thing.* Walter took out his wallet, laid down twenty dollars and stood up.

"It's been nice talking with you," Walter said, "but I have to meet a friend."

Sta-fon gave him a sad smile and looked at him directly; his eyes were green again, the green of new leaves.

On MacDougal the snow was icy and coming hard. Ice had already encased the evergreen, naked now and lying on the sidewalk. He felt his heart throb and his body felt fragile and empty, like a delicate glass vase. Fuck Sta-fon and his love of middlebrow novels. He headed down Sullivan toward the Two Potato.

His rage flew out and attached to objects. He hated the red gloves in a store window; he hated the cold that made his cheeks burn and bit through the thin material of his pastor pants. He hated the ridges of dirty snow and the sky; he really hated the sky which was completely starless. He saw two men holding hands. He hated them. He saw a man and a woman holding hands. He hated them. He saw an older man walking his dog; he hated the man for living so long and he hated the stupid little terrier that continued to shiver even though it wore a kelly green sweater.

Inside, the bar was warm and barely lit, and Walter felt relieved, as if he'd been covered over with a layer of warm earth. The scent of sweat and gin was like a tranquilizer, and even the red carpet, covered with a constellation of cigarette burns, was comforting. Mirrors covered the walls and a few stray bits of disco-ball light flew over the bar like flakes of ghostly snow. He ordered a Jack Daniel's straight up and looked around the bar.

Businessmen in button-down shirts and loafers clustered around the jukebox; a German man in leather gazed at the blond boy dancing alone. This place was definitely holy. Mostly because of the longing. God loved longing and imbued it with sanctity. All through his life, things outside the church were just as holy as the crosses and statues inside: rain and hard rain particularly, which made his mother's apartment cozy and complete; his book of fables with the picture of the sad lion with a thorn in his paw; the way, on youth group retreats, Silk read a Jane Austen novel out loud as he drank cognac from a tiny red glass. In high school the janitor had taken him down to see the furnace. The gray-haired man had swung open the metal door and Walter had felt he was getting a glimpse of eternity. Carlos's body was definitely holy, his black chest hairs, and the way his hip bones stuck out from his pelvis.

The ice cubes dissolved into his last swallow of bourbon. Fuck Sta-fon and his love of Cajun cooking. The bartender, unseasonably tan in a tight mesh tank top, asked if he wanted another. Walter nodded and watched the blond boy sway on the dance floor. His eyes were closed and his face freaked with disco-ball light.

Just the thing against the other thing. In this case the blond boy's cock against his taste buds and, really, there wasn't much else to report, Walter thought, not drunkenly exactly but definitely from another room in the heavenly mansion, one filled with black glitter and gnaw. He opened one eye, saw the young man's white tennis shoes near his knees and how the black light in the Two Potato's back room scintillated bits of lint on his jeans.

The motion of the young man's pelvis sped up. *Just the thing against the other thing.* Just the bottom of a glass against a wood table or a chair pressed up against a wall. *The thing against the other thing,* that was the most human of all, the most embodied, not flesh infused with spirit. No. *Just the thing against the other thing.* It was holy no matter how sleazy the circumstance, as it was the sensation beyond the reach of God. The feel of soft hair against his lips made him see colors: green and pink as he hung in the dark; the black light showing white buttons on one man's shirt; and the yellow beads around the neck of another.

Just the thing against the other thing. Walter tried to remember Carlos's body. His black hair and brown eyes. His lankiness. When he laughed his dark eyebrows rose up in his forehead and his mouth opened. But dead people, no matter how fascinating, didn't hold up in fantasies. Carlos had no body. His physical form was ash, ash in a canister Walter kept under his bed, and so in reality to fuck Carlos would be to fuck dust, which could be like fucking God. But before that thought got him anywhere, the young man came salty and acidic as a margarita, and Walter felt many things, including degradation and peace.

Two

THE ALEPH HAD come to represent to Mary an outward manifestation of her soul. For a while Walter was fascinated by how she claimed to have seen her mother as a girl chasing a chicken on one shiny disk and on another a lady watching television. There were on other disks noisy baby birds waiting for their breakfast and a nighttime parking lot. Not to mention the dead boy with red running out of his nostrils, and the white tulip moving slowly back and forth on the tiny circular screen.

But after a few weeks of her insisting on talking about the aleph over breakfast and dinner, as well as bringing it up in front of Mr. Cabalaro, the head of the church trustees, Walter was growing frustrated. He explained to her how, when the present became unbearable, the brain's happy hideout was the supernatural. He urged her to wean the baby and get on the pills, but she refused. Seeing his discomfort, she tried to replicate the aleph using tiny mirrors she found in a store on Canal Street and suspending them with dental floss from the ceiling of her room. In the evening, after extinguishing the lamp, she shined a flashlight on the glass slivers and described the internal sensation that accompanied the sightings. A sucking sensation, as if her heart were sucked by the nozzle of a vacuum, and mental deterioration, similar to the mind's assignations on mushrooms, the brain's surface texture changing from hard metal to something damp and porous like bread.

She was becoming, even Walter had to admit, a sort of spooky chick with her delicate frame, its angular elegance akin to a skeleton's and her limp hair hanging around her face. A dozen times he found her praying inside the closet. She seemed to prefer the one on the third floor where he had first found her, but he also discovered her inside the kitchen pantry, kneeling among cans of tomato juice and rolls of paper towels.

Mary said she needed to talk to him, and he decided that if she started up about the aleph, he was going to suggest again that she wean the baby and get on the pills. It wasn't that he didn't believe her. He did. But if God wasn't going to make his message known, there was nothing Mary could do to force it.

He'd known other people who got obsessed. One, a pale southern boy in seminary, was fixated on kudzu, its viscous growth pattern and how the noxious vine infiltrated America. Walter remembered how, in Old Testament class, this young man always tried to use kudzu as a metaphor for God's motivations in biblical narratives. The other was a cousin, who, after John Lennon was murdered, became convinced that his spirit inhabited all cellular life, so that even a blender had qualities of the most complicated Beatle, as did her tennis shoes.

He looked up and there was Mary walking down the stairs. She seemed thinner, less materially substantial, as if thousands of her atoms had disintegrated. Walter stood.

"Is his fever better?"

"I gave him a little Tylenol," she said, taking the chair by the fireplace. Walter sat across from her on the couch. He glanced at his watch; he was having dinner with the bishop at eight.

Flitting her hands around, she talked about the

renovation schedule. The painting that still needed to be done, the work she and Junot had already accomplished and what they hoped to do by working consistently through Lent.

"But that's not what you wanted to talk about?" Walter said.

"No," she said. "I want to ask you if you think it's possible to break into time?"

Walter blinked. "How do you mean?"

Mary looked at him. "Let's say a tiny animal, a squirrel or a chipmunk, had, encoded in its very DNA, in its skeleton, the equation that would stop time and bring about a Second Coming."

Walter watched her face carefully; he tried to imagine he was watching Hildegard or Mathilde, any of the early mystics who had experienced God firsthand.

"It's possible, right, if we find the right posture, the correct way to hold our skeleton, the door between this dimension and the next will fly open and there'll be only the slightest difference in density between myself and my dead mother?" She paused and looked directly at him, in an effort, Walter knew, to guage his reaction.

He knew these ideas were somehow connected not only

to the aleph sighting but also to her weekly visits with the monk. What transpired between them Mary never let on, though she came home wanting to talk about the spiritual connection between making music and feeding the poor. She was an odd sight with her strained features and her hair half-black and half-blond. She hadn't dyed it since she had found out she was pregnant and so there were a good six inches of black at the roots, and she seemed to be wearing the same jeans every day and either her gray sweatshirt or her blue one.

He understood what fueled her longing. It was unconscionable to live separated from God, like a cork held under water; the urge for union was often untenable. But what Mary wanted was technically impossible: to feel God's touch physically manifested.

"What you're saying is interesting, and I don't doubt what you suspect is true. If one believes in a divine presence that connects everything, a fine web of interrelatedness, then inside any object, be it a squirrel or a refrigerator, resides particles of eternity."

Mary sat forward; she pressed her hands together, threading her fingers. He imagined he could see the green tiles on the fireplace behind her right through her forehead.

"And I can understand both your desire for unification with the Godhead and the hope that time might give way to infinity."

"So you don't think it's possible?" Mary said, looking into the fireplace filled with ash. Her face had clouded over.

He knew from reading saints' biographies that there was always a point of disassociation from reality, from the material world; there was, as doctors would say, the schizophrenic break that led either to the asylum or to greater knowledge. Joan of Arc's vision of the Virgin gave her the courage to go to war, and Walter had just read about a woman who, after her mental collapse, wore an apron with "THE PILGRIM" spelled out in felt letters. She walked miles with a radiant smile on her face and spoke to anyone who would listen about saving the earth.

"That's not what I'm saying," Walter said. "I'm saying that what you suspect is happening all the time. Just think about the crazy foliage God sends up in the spring, those green tulip tentacles coming up out of the dead leaves, and what about snow?" He gestured to the window. "For God's sake, look at it." He held his hand high as if directing the tiny bits of crystallized ice. Flakes moved as they had all winter past the bay window in a gentle and glittering trajectory.

"See what I mean?"

"I guess," she said, deflated. "You think I'm being too literal."

Walter shook his head. "No, I think you're not being literal enough. I mean religion insists on paradox. Everything is wonderful. Everything is terrible. Both at the same time. That's how it is with everything, degradation and divinity, the material and the corporeal, all unified so on one level a blade of grass is an everyday object, but in another way it's a supernatural thing."

Mary hung her head; she was clearly disappointed, and he could tell this by the way she'd rested her hands, fingers spread, on her knees.

"I understand my soul is like a piece of God implanted in me, and while it's the same substance as God, it's much more cloudy because it's so hard to be human."

Walter stared at her. In her own way, he thought, Mary was spiritually advanced.

THREE

Bishop Silk wore his white cap and biretta, the
latter at a jaunty angle like an artist's beret. He was
elfin and smiley, and there was something oozy about him,
as if between his skin and musculature was a layer of
molasses. Walter watched him talk as the red wine hit his
system and an aura formed around the restaurant's chan-
delier and the paisleys on the wallpaper shifted like
tadpoles.

Silk complained about his nemesis, the New Jersey
bishop, who was so poisoned by New Age philosophy he'd
led a joint retreat with a space alien expert. Things in the
dioceses had been crazy. *I've been putting out flames right
and left.* A priest up in Inwood had fired off a round from
the rectory back door, and another down in the Village

got caught having sex in the sacristy. *Thank God, in both cases we kept the press out of it.*

Silk sighed as two steaks, bruised blue with peppercorn cream and mashed potatoes, were set down before them and the heavyset waiter with the red face poured more cabernet into their goblets, joking that they didn't need to worry, the cook had blessed the bottle in back. Silk grinned and tipped his head coquettishly. He'd always been equal parts Liberace and Saint Sebastian. Walter watched his pale blue eyes as he chewed; his cincture was embroidered with glittery red thread. Walter touched the notebook in his pocket; he had all the figures neatly written out but he didn't know how to get started.

"You don't look good, Walty."

Walter cringed at his old nickname. He'd asked Silk not to use it. But after the incident with the boy uptown, *Walty* had reappeared. Silk's gaze was unnerving; his pale eyes like water.

"I read that Walter Wink book," Walter said.

"What'd you think of it?" Silk asked. Like a lot of religious people Walter knew, Silk wasn't particularly interested in theology.

"I like the idea that everything good that happens in the world is rooted in prayer."

"That is a nice idea," Silk said.

"And that there is no part of creation that hasn't been redeemed."

Silk looked at him, then motioned to the waiter. "Can we have more of that delicious sourdough bread?"

Walter felt the notebook in his pocket; he better speak up before he said anything stupid again.

"We're short again this month."

The bishop's face stiffened. Walter recognized the expression from earlier times: when he'd told him about first meeting Carlos on Fire Island, and the time before in seminary, when he'd had his crisis of faith. The bishop was known for his communication skills, but Walter noticed that there were certain impenetrable subjects the bishop was not willing to discuss.

Walter continued. "The heating bill alone is higher than a whole month's collection."

The bishop stabbed a piece of steak with his fork and swung it back and forth in the cream sauce. "What about the money I gave you in September?"

"The leak in the roof wiped that out. The whole ceiling

had to be plastered. If you could float us one more month the stewardship committee is planning a phone-a-thon at Easter."

"What about Newberry?"

"I went to see her last week. Blessed her cat, looked at her photos of Tuscany, the whole nine yards."

The bishop smiled and held his eyebrows up. "I'd go over and talk to her again. Be more explicit this time."

"Do you want me to beg her?" His voice sounded angry, but he didn't care, remembering how Mrs. Newberry had gone into the kitchen to *get him something* but returned with a package of pasta instead of her checkbook.

"I thought you understood, Walty. You need to make a go of it out there," he said as he reached in his pocket for his wallet and took out three hundred-dollar bills. "This is a gift, Walty. But I am deeply disappointed. Your mother would roll over in her grave if she could see you at this point."

Walter thought of his mother sleeping in their tiny Queens apartment; in her polyester nightgown she had snored away on the foldout couch.

Walter was in a light-headed state of postcoital bliss as he lay beside the blond boy on his narrow twin bed. After he left the bishop, he'd found the boy at the Two Potato, and they'd come over here. The radiator in the corner hummed reassuringly, and he looked past the slats of the fire escape to the darkened apartment building across the alley. One window showed a gingham potholder hanging over a stove. The boy slept in a flannel shirt and his body smelled like wet dirt. He shifted and asked Walter if he was okay; he said it so sweetly, his breath against Walter's collarbone, that he turned to the boy and began kissing him again. His cock hardened against Walter's leg; his testicles were huge, each like a brown egg. Physically, he was nothing like Carlos, but his earnestness was similar. And he was a good kisser, understanding that kissing was all about the nuance of touch rather than touch itself.

"What do you do, anyway?" the boy whispered. "I mean for money."

"I sell insurance."

"Oh." He was clearly disappointed. Walter remembered that earlier the boy had said he studied Sanskrit.

In an effort to make up for his dull profession, Walter slid down between the boy's legs and ran his tongue up the length of his cock. The boy's fingers moved through his hair and pressed Walter's head into his pelvis. After a while the boy came, and Walter lay back down and looked up at the ceiling. He remembered how Silk had wiped the corners of his mouth with his linen napkin and pushed his chair out from the table. A crack near the far wall resembled an octopus tentacle, and the light in the alley was extinguished so the objects in the room looked vague and mysterious, like algae-covered refuse lying on the bottom of the sea. The bourbon was wearing off, and Walter held his white arm straight up in the dark room.

When he got home Mary's door was ajar. In the slant of light from the hallway he saw the baby in his terry-cloth sleeper and Mary lying fully clothed beside him, asleep but at an odd angle, legs akimbo and arms out like a drunken sailor. In the corner where her aleph had hung, now bits of masking tape dipped down from the ceiling. He saw, too, that she'd stacked the small mirrors on top of her chest in little columns like spare change.

Four

HE HAD THREE distinct headaches: one above his right ear, another below his left temple and the third, and worst, like a burr embedded in his brain tissue. The text for Sunday was the Bible story of Jonah, son of Amittai. When he was young the story of Jonah had been Walter's favorite: the boat pitching wildly, the sailors casting lots to see who had pissed God off. Now he was more interested in Jonah's three days in the belly of the whale, the smell of salt and the feel of moist membrane. He remembered the slant of alley from the boy's window, the flakes of snow and the boy's yeasty breath. He wanted to write his own parables, more contemporary than the ones in the Gospels, but just as mysterious. In one, a man in a blue sweater would fall asleep on the subway and wake up in a green house surrounded by oak trees. In another, a child's toy plane was equipped with a bathing car where men took showers. There was the one about the old woman sitting in her yard contemplating a silver handbag, and in yet another, a little brown dog sat on top of a dirty blanket.

There was a knock, and the door pushed open. Junot handed him the mail, a church supply catalogue and another electric bill. Walter ripped open the envelope; if he didn't pay by Friday, St. Paul's electricity would be turned off. Walter reached for the list of chores he'd written out on an index card. Junot wore his usual baggy low-rider pants and an oversize Knicks jersey, "Sprewell" spelled out on the back. He stood just inside the doorway, looking past Walter's head out the window to the snowy back garden.

"The rug on the altar needs to be vacuumed, and if you have time, will you break down the crèche?"

Junot nodded, but he didn't move. "Did you ever feel evil, Father?"

"On occasion," Walter said. "That goes with being human."

"My mother says I'm evil."

"Why would she say such a thing?"

"She says '*De tal palo, tal astilla—que se hereda de los padres.*' She thinks I get it from my father."

Walter looked at the boy carefully. He wore his oversize shirt and pants ironically and his hair, which Walter always assumed was a lucky accident of nature, now appeared to be arranged with lots of hair gel.

"Luckily, God is a lot more understanding than most mothers."

Junot's face brightened.

"Nothing against your mother, Junot, but her religious ideas have always seemed a little strange."

"You think so?" Junot said.

Walter nodded. "I do."

Mrs. Newberry's gray hair was short, and she was fragile as a dry leaf as she floated around her massive brownstone, turning on the lamp with the cream silk shade and bringing him a cup of chamomile tea.

"I'm exhausted," she said flinging herself down on the velvet couch. Mrs. Newberry conducted tours for school-children at the Brooklyn Museum. She wore the docent uniform: a khaki skirt and white turtleneck. Buttercup jumped onto her lap, and she began petting the cat's neck, staring down into the strains of white fur.

"It must be tiring," Walter said. He sat on the edge of a brocade wing-backed chair.

"I assume this isn't a social call," Newberry said.

"Well. No." Walter had hoped they'd have a few minutes of casual conversation before he asked for the money. "Bishop Silk suggested I visit you."

Newberry raised her eyebrows and continued petting her cat in long, languid strokes.

"I was wondering, I mean, we were wondering if you might want to make a donation." He felt his face get hot.

"To what exactly?" Newberry said.

"The church, our building. We're in rather dire straits."

"How much were you thinking of?"

"Five thousand?"

"That's an awful lot of money, Walter."

"Three thousand then?" He hated the pleading quality in his voice.

"You know Chase Bank let my daughter go. So I'm helping out there."

"Oh, I'm sorry to hear Christine lost her job." He hoped he'd gotten the daughter's name right.

"I also pay my grandchildren's private school tuition."

"That is generous of you," Walter said.

She looked out the bay window. The lower Manhattan skyscrapers hung above the choppy East River.

"Why do you think our people aren't giving?"

"Oh, I don't know," Walter said. "The economy is bad."

"I don't think the economy has anything to do with it."

"Then what?"

"Your sermons are rather depressing. Don't you think? I mean, every week do we have to hear about racism and the poor?"

Walter looked down at his hands. He would not defend himself.

"Coming from you, I think people feel it's a bit much."

Did she mean because he was gay? Or because of the boy from the church in Manhattan? He didn't think she knew about that, but Walter realized she meant it more generally. Newberry felt he was diseased, spiritually diseased. He stared at the Chinese vase on the end table.

"I'll try and do better," he said.

"That's my boy," Newberry said as she pulled her checkbook out of her purse and began to scribble with a ballpoint pen.

Walter needed a drink. He still hadn't finished his sermon, but inspiration would have to come at the bar. So he brought his notebook to the Two Potato and tried to formulate ideas on Jonah. Tomorrow morning, Mrs. Newberry would be sitting in the front pew. He could think of things to say about Jonah's confinement inside the whale—how it was key to cultivate the difficult; that adventure was just misfortune correctly understood—but whether these ideas would fit in with Mrs. Newberry's idea of the spiritual plane was impossible to calculate.

For the first drink he had the notebook open, the pen beside the wire spiral, but by the second he closed the notebook and shoved it into the pocket of his coat. He'd never been this unprepared on a Saturday night before his Sunday sermon. Guilt bloomed in his chest with every tick of the Felix the Cat clock that beat over the bar's cash register. He knew he should go home, but the Sanskrit boy haunted him—how his cock tasted slightly of metal, as if a roll of tinfoil had phoned up from Kansas. He couldn't get the sensation out of his mouth. He searched the guys in tight jeans gathered around the dance floor; all had faces smooth as ceramic saint statues.

There was no physical resemblance between the Sanskrit boy and Carlos. Carlos had olive skin and was Walter's age. The similarity was all in the boy's countenance. The way the Sanskrit boy leaned a little to the side as if uninfluenced by the rules of gravity. He'd seen orderlies roll Carlos off on a gurney after he died, and he'd picked up his ashes at the crematorium. But he couldn't really believe Carlos was dead. His soul had flown to God but his physical qualities had been infused into everything, one man's long eyelashes, another's chaotic hand movements. Once Walter saw a pigeon cock his head in a gesture reminiscent of Carlos and, another time, saw a branch shift in the wind, the same way that Carlos, when surprised, swayed back on his heels. Carlos commingled with everything. Walter sensed his presence but could not touch him, and this made Walter lonely and morose.

He ordered a martini and as the bartender turned away pulled his sweater back over his shoulders and looked to see if anybody had noticed he was wearing his clerical. But the sparse late-night crowd were round eyed, red faced and mostly wasted. Shame expanded and floated around inside his heart. Newberry was right; there was something wrong with him. He thought of the Sanskrit boy's bed and took out his notebook and wrote the Sanskrit boy a letter which spoke of God and *the thing against the other thing*. And how Carlos had seen divinity in everything, the stained-glass window as well as the Styrofoam cup. He explained about the other boy, the high school boy from the church in Manhattan. The narrowness of his shoulders, his striped rugby shirt, the fact that at fourteen, he could speak perfect French. He tried to articulate why he'd become a pastor: *Because at first I assumed the church held the same cozy qualities as your bedroom.*

He looked up and saw a man standing at the edge of the dance floor, his hand wrapped around a brown bottle of beer. Walter found the man's wispy haircut and jean jacket devastatingly erotic, but after staring for a while, he gave up trying to catch his eye. Besides himself, there was only one other man sitting at the bar, a stocky fellow who clearly had hair transplants. Walter could see the plugs of hair like seedlings across his head. He wore a green sweater with an insignia and gazed at the men moving around on the multicolored dance floor.

The door opened, and the Karaoke King of Chelsea came into the bar. Walter loved how he wore his silk scarf and leather jacket. Last call. Another martini with four olives, one for each of the Gospels. As he listened in on the conversation between the King and the fat man, he ate the olives. Talk turned to Ankara. The King took out a picture of the Rui Madria ripped from *National Geographic*, and the fat man bragged about the cheap brandy and anisette he bought in Tristaina last spring. *It was impossible*, the Karaoke King said, *to visit Tristaina in spring because of monsoon season and mud slides*. The conversation turned hostile, and the King slapped the fat man, jumped off his stool and ran out the front door and into the night.

The fat man looked after him, his wet lips trembling, then put his face down so his cheek rested on the bar. Walter walked over and placed his hand on the back of the man's head. His fat face streaked with water, and they watched snow whiz past the front window. A gust of wind flipped a woman's umbrella and she was pulled across the street.

Outside, new snow made a flat sound on the heels of Walter's shoes, and at the corner the mixed dirt and snow looked like cookie dough. The fat man's long sideburns framed his sullen features, and he wore a thin windbreaker, though the temperature was below freezing. Walter lit a cigarette and asked the fat man questions, but he just nodded and shrugged. *Where are you from?* got the same nod-shrug combination as *I guess you're not in a talkative mood?*

Their watery reflection in storefront windows was illusive and glamorous, and when he turned into an alley Walter realized with a thrill that the fat man wanted to have sex. At the end of the alley was a Dumpster filled with cardboard and the man seemed familiar with a patch of snowless cement, warmed by a dryer vent.

Walter tried to kiss the man's mouth, but his lips felt dry and muscular, and he could tell the man did not like kissing. He fumbled for the man's cock inside his dress pants and as he located it, knelt. The man's hand moved into Walter's hair; he liked his hair stroked while he gave head, but then the fingers fisted, and Walter felt individual hairs pulled loose from their sockets as the man took hold of his cock and pointed the soft tip directly at Walter's heart.

A spasm of repulsion shot through his body. But then he felt the cold asphalt through the material of his preacher pants, and he heard the sound of a thousand bits of ice falling onto the metal lid of the Dumpster. *Just let me take my coat off.* He was shaking as he kneeled down again in front of the fat man, eye level now with his groin. Warm air tinged with the scent of fabric softener spilled out from the dryer vent as the fat man again took hold of Walter's hair, but this time more gently. The urine made a flat sound and was warm and then cold against his shirt.

FIVE

WALTER'S DAMP SHIRT was icy against his chest as he glanced up at the blue television light that illuminated the rectangular window of the Sanskrit boy's apartment. Certain details interested him immensely. The little potato that sat in a muddy patch of snow near the curb. Particular snowflakes. He'd fixate on the trajectory of one until it seesawed down and obliterated itself on the pavement. An aura seemed to be coming off everything; the streetlights of course, but also a mailbox and a pair of polar-fleece mittens in a store window.

A man in a knit cap passed by, and Walter pretended fascination with a flyer advertising massages tacked up to the tree across from the boy's building. Walter cataloged bits of foil on the ground and loose cassette tape in the crease of the curb. His hands were freezing and he couldn't stop shivering, nor could he stop thinking about the boy's warm bed: the blue sheets with little butterflies on them and how his comforter and pillow were stuffed with duck-feather down. A light went on in a brownstone and he realized he'd spoken out loud. A tall woman with black hair and a long robe clenched at the waist looked at him severely, and he crossed the street and rang the boy's bell. He was buzzed in immediately. *The boy had seen him from the window! The boy would be waiting with a shy smile and a cup of chamomile tea!*

In the elevator he decided he needed an excuse. He'd say he'd left his scarf, the cashmere one he'd bought last year in India. But he had his scarf on, the five-dollar one he'd bought on the street last week; so he yanked it from around his neck and shoved it deep down into his pocket. The apartment door was open and he walked briskly down the hallway into the boy's living room.

It was dark—there was only the gray light from the television and the sound of a woman's voice speaking in French. Denim legs entwined on the couch; Walter realized the Sanskrit boy was lying with someone else. The boy glanced behind him, lazily holding out a twenty-dollar bill. His eyes widened as he recognized Walter, and he jumped up.

"Can I use your bathroom?" Walter sputtered.

"No," the boy said, "I thought you were the pizza guy. That's why the door was—"

"Oh, let him," the other boy said. He had a long soulful face and was sitting up now in the lotus position. "It's at the end of the hall."

There was a film around the hole in the toilet and a lacy frost on the sink spigot. The shower curtain hung off the rod and a little jade Buddha lay facedown in the soap dish. He heard the two boys arguing as he flushed the toilet and ran water into the sink.

Outside the bathroom, Walter felt himself sucked down the hallway and onto the boy's bed. He lay in the dark, the comforter cool against his body, watching snow fall into the alley over the silver radiator. He heard footsteps and the overhead light flipped on and the Sanskrit boy's face was red with rage.

"What the fuck are you doing?"

Walter was going to sit up and say that he felt better now, that he had a condition the doctors could never quite diagnose, part low blood sugar, part narcolepsy. But instead he just closed his eyes and pretended to sleep. The boy stood there a minute and then pressed the numbers on his cell phone and spoke into the receiver. The other boy came and stood beside him, and both stared down.

Walter slit his eyes just enough to see the pale orb of the Sanskrit boy's head.

Snow was slanted against the windows of the parsonage kitchen and the little yard was blanketed; just the tips of the azalea bush pressed up over the full line of snow. Walter still smelled of piss and his arm ached from where the Sanskrit boy had yanked him up off the bed. He walked with his glass of ice water and stood in the living room. There was a shape on the couch and at first he thought his eye was superimposing the scene from earlier tonight, Sanskrit boy and brown-haired boy melded together on the couch.

"Father, my mother kicked me out," Junot said, sitting up. "Mary said I could sleep here."

"That's fine," Walter said. "Are you warm enough?"

Junot motioned to the blanket Mary had gotten from the hall closet. "It was awful, Father," he said. "She said I was just like my dad. She kept saying '*Arbol que crece torcido jamás su tronco endereza—cuando algo empieza mal, termina mal*,' and that I was a crook and a bloodsucker." The boy's white T-shirt glowed in the dark room. And Walter saw out the window how snow was piled up on the boxwoods so that they looked like angel food cakes. "She threw my boom box out the window and said I was going to hell." Junot's teeth were white as sour cream and the expanse of his eyes was a liquid black.

"It sounds terrible."

"I guess I give her problems," Junot said sadly.

"Get some sleep now," Walter said as he moved up the stairs. He wore only his underwear, and his cock was getting hard. An ice cube in his drink cracked. "In the morning, we'll shovel."

"Thank you, Father," Junot said.

Walter rolled over, pressed himself into the mattress and covered the back of his head with a pillow. *Junot's lips, his eyebrows, the baby hairs at the nape of his neck. The way his jeans rode low on his hips.* His skin was milky brown and he smelled like Carlos, crème soda and black pepper. Walter couldn't take it anymore and stood up by the side of his bed. He put his hands on his hips. Snow rushed past the window, the darkness offsetting the chaotic pattern of rushing white.

Walter kneeled down and pulled out the enamel canister. The lid stuck at first, but by using the file on his nail clipper, he levered the top off, and there, in a plastic bag tied with a twisty, was what remained of Carlos. He looked at the white ash and bits of gray bone matter.

That people you loved died was unacceptable. Also that people you fucked wanted you to vanish was unacceptable. But really it was mostly that people you loved died—this was completely unacceptable.

He sat the canister on the nightstand and lit a cigarette, blew out a tendril of smoke. Carlos had been explicit about his ashes; he wanted them scattered down by Bargemusic. Walter had been putting it off, but as soon as it got light he decided to walk down to the bridge. He thought of the ashes floating down into the East River, the fine gray dust burnt clean and pure.

PART III

JOHN

ONE

JOHN SHAVED OFF his beard, then laid his surplice out on the bed along with the gold ring the order gave him when he'd taken his vow. He moved around his cell slowly. He was worried about rousing Brother Peter, with whom he shared a bathroom and who was a notoriously light sleeper.

He'd been winnowing his possessions for weeks and had just a stack of old letters secured with a rubber band, an envelope of money he'd saved from his weekly allowance and the crucifix that had hung over his bed. He wore khakis, a white button-down and his tennis shoes as he walked down the long hallway past the meditation garden with the dogwood tree and wood benches and through the common room, where the *New York Times* lay on the round table alongside the *Christian Science Monitor*. He saw the stone hand that sat on a side table and the photo of the order's monastery in Zimbabwe.

The ratty velvet couch, the bronze lamp with the linen shade, the worn oriental, everything was soaked through with incense and loneliness, and he couldn't wait to get out. The carpet runner ended and his tennis shoes squelched against the wood. He went up on tiptoe as he passed the kitchen door. He knew Mac was inside preparing the monks' breakfast.

Mac looked more like a wizard than a monk with his long gray hair and beard. He'd worked most of his life in a leprosorium in Africa, and when John first came to Holy Cross, he'd sat next to him at meals listening to Mac's stories: the legless girl who rolled around on a wheeled pedestal and the old man with a face so disfigured he wore a hood with eye slits. The central symbol of Mac's life was the round communion wafer lying in the palm of a leper's hand.

As quiet as he tried to be, the door swung open and he was blinded with fluorescent light.

"John?" Mac said. "You're going?"

"I'm sorry."

"No need to apologize," he said, smiling. "Let me accompany you up the hill."

John had expected Mac to be angry or at least disappointed, but he wasn't going to try and convince John to stay or mention the fantasy woman. Mac had said John's fantasy girl was a robot, an idealized notion of romantic love, impossible to replicate. But now, Mac seemed to realize the woman had won. Mac walked beside him up the long asphalt drive. The trunks of the trees around them were black and creaked in the breeze. John wanted to say something, but the raw reality of what he was about to do rendered him speechless. He kept his hands deep in his empty pockets and his eyes on the white tips of his tennis shoes. At the end of the drive, the red taxi waited, "Brown Sugar" blasting out the windows. When the driver saw them he turned down the radio.

"I'll write you."

"No you won't," Mac said.

"I will," John insisted, concentrating on the first line of gray light at the horizon. He had failed as a monk; he had not let himself become absorbed into the monastic life; out of insecurity, he had tried to protect his identity.

Mac opened the car door and John threw his bag inside. "What should I tell the others?" he asked.

"That I'm sorry," John said as he sank down into the backseat and pulled the door closed. His chest felt thick and achy. The driver turned the Stones back up and pulled out onto the highway. John looked back at Mac drenched in reflected red light.

The backseat of the cab reeked of smoke and the beige vinyl was sticky, details that seemed to foreshadow the chaos and shabbiness of his new life. *My God, my God, why have you forsaken me?* The car sped down the highway toward the band of yellow at the horizon, and John lay his cheek against the cold window flecked with tiny drops of water. God's voice came back to him. *So you can know yourself.*

The first week outside the monastery, car alarms, garbage trucks, the subway, all grated on his tender nerves. Women on the city streets hurt him with their fragile preoccupied features. He missed the bells that had rung every few hours, and the offices haunted him, vespers in particular. The monks' plainsong was loud inside his head. At first he felt his fifteen years in the monastery had been wasted, but then he realized that constant prayer had honed his perceptions. He saw that nothing was wholly static; color hummed with a kind of energy. He noted each individual leaf on each individual tree. Every person on the street sent out a delicate aura.

He rented a studio in Brooklyn Heights and began in the evening to go to a bar on Court Street, a generic place called Murphy's. There the television blasted football games and the regulars were mostly red-faced men and a few slack-faced ladies who laughed too loud. He'd been drawn to a petite Hispanic woman who had, when he approached, explained curtly that she wanted to be left alone. At Bar Tabac, the woman with feather earrings said she was waiting for her boyfriend, and at Churchill's, the attractive lady in the business suit told him she was gay. Similar scenarios resulted in all the watering holes around Brooklyn Heights.

He was frustrated and usually woke with a hard-on that was biblical in its intensity. Sometimes he masturbated, but afterward he always felt depressed. One day he picked up a *Village Voice* and flipped to the ads in the back. *Cheap Sluts. Hot Local Girls. Live One-on-One Action.* The thonged rear ends and cleavage stimulated him, but he'd be too shy for phone sex.

The listings under *Adult Body Work* confused him. The pictures were flagrant, women's hands cupping their surgically enhanced breasts and pulling back the cheeks of their rear ends to show their anuses. There was only one ad that appealed to him. *Kathy*, a blonde in a white nightgown standing before a fireplace. *Outcalls Only*, the ad said, and John assumed this meant she'd come to his place.

The money was sealed in an envelope on the mantel and he poured brandy into two teacups. He'd showered, shaved and dressed carefully in his khakis and white button-down. When the buzzer rang the woman who walked down the stairs was not the Kathy from the picture. This Kathy had thick reddish hair, cut full at the top with long straight pieces coming down against her neck. Her eyes were huge and brown and her lips full but flat. She wore a leather miniskirt with metal studs and a tight black blouse. Her accent was Slavic with some New Jersey underneath. He felt his face get warm as she went over the economics of their endeavor.

John watched her walk to the futon, pull off her boots and spread her legs, exposing the crotch of her black panties. John assumed there'd be conversation, but he appeared to be mistaken, as he watched the woman arch her back and look at him with her mouth open. Her underwear was slick, the skin around the black material pink and hairless. He walked over to the futon and removed his shoes. His tennis shoes looked pathetic. Kathy pulled at his arm and he lay down beside her. He noticed that in the center of her right eyebrow was a patch of white hair.

"Do you want to fuck me?" Kathy said. She sounded like Natasha from the Bullwinkle cartoon. He closed his eyes and nodded. Kathy undid his pants, loosened his cock and crawled backward; her mouth was warm and wet as she moved her head. He thrust his penis up toward her face and opened his eyes. Kathy's head moved up and down like the needle in a sewing machine, and her eyes were open, the pupils dilated big as dimes. On the nape of her neck was a small scar. Pleasure had been rerouted over humanity and he wanted to try and change that.

"How did you get your scar?" He touched the raised pink flesh.

Kathy jerked her head to look at him. She was clearly annoyed. "It's a scar."

"I know," John said. "How did you get it?"

"Oh somehow, I can't remember now," Kathy said, moving her wet mouth toward his crotch.

Two

A LUMP OF CREAM cheese, crackers and a little bottle of capers; this was his last dinner at the Heights apartment. He ate on his futon; everything else was in boxes. He figured the car service could haul his possessions out to Sunset Park.

Opening his journal, John turned to the pages at the end, which were clean and white. He'd gotten a brief note from Holy Cross asking if he wanted to be exclaustrated, released from his vow, and he'd been thinking all day about what to write. "Dear Mac," he began, but then thought of addressing the letter to the whole community. No. The only brother he felt any real affection for was Mac.

Dear Mac:

I would like to be exclaustrated. I may be called back some day to Holy Cross, but I was called out. I want to make this clear to you. I don't know if you can accept it, but God did call me out, and those visions I had of a woman, a partner, both sexually and domestically, have been to some extent realized. I don't want to go into too much detail, but I want you to know that I understand now what you used to say about God only being able to see Love, that it was philosophically impossible for God to even think about evil, that Love was all and we must make ourselves into vehicles of Love. I know you feel romantic love cannot accommodate the detachment that compassion demands. But I want to tell you that at this moment, as fraught as it is for me (for reasons I cannot yet discuss), a bigger portion of me, of my being, my soul, whatever you want to call it, has been changed into Love than was true at any time I was in the monastery.

Give my regards to the brothers and I want you to know that you are ever in my thoughts. When I left Holy Cross I thought I'd get away from your edicts, but it appears now that the real reason I left was so that I could embody them more fully.

Yours,

John

He read over the letter and put in a P.S. about Molly the monastery dog. He was pleased with what he'd written and ripped the page out of his journal, addressed an envelope and leaned the letter on the mantel. He lay down on the futon; the comforter was already packed, so he pulled his coat up to his shoulders. He watched snow fall at the curtainless window; the flakes were big, and it must have gotten colder, for they were sticking, gathering on the sidewalk and in the rents of the wrought-iron fence. He lay there with his eyes closed, occasionally looking up and out the window and thinking. Darkness overtook him and at some point he began to dream.

The Dog Star hung like a radiant ice cube in the black sky. Bits of ice hit the back of his ankles as he passed a jewelry store; its windows were empty of merchandise. He saw the dog moving along the sidewalk on the other side of the street. The mutt's fur was ratty and tiny headlights shone out from each of his eyes. John followed the dog down an alley, long and white and warm. The alley narrowed and John had to squeeze his body sideways, his nose grazing the bricks. At the end he saw the velvet chair from the monastery and he knew by a strain of hair, half-black, half-blond, that he'd just missed Mary.

He heard a noise and opened his eyes to the glowing numbers on the clock. The veridescent numbers rolled on the seventies clock radio and he felt his heart like a water balloon in a metal vise. He craved her. Mac had warned against this. Mac argued for detachment, and that was reasonable when talking about middle-aged brothers but not Mary whom he wanted to imbibe; he wanted to taste her spit and put his tongue up inside her.

He sat against the wall, squeezed his eyes shut and tried to find that dark shining passage of peace, but it was like an elusive dock, unanchored in night water. He tried the Jesus Prayer. *Lord have mercy on me.* And then the Lord's Prayer. Neither helped. He thought again of walking over to the rectory, but this was impossible. She had said she wasn't ready to see him. If he knocked on her door in the middle of the night, he'd seem both pathetic and insane.

He turned on the lamp and picked up the baby book. He was learning about diaper rash and what foods were hard on a baby's stomach, about how to deal with night-time crying and pink eye. He read about how to make homemade baby food by mixing mother's milk and sweet potatoes. He read about homeopathic cures for ear infections and how babies need fewer baths during cold months.

He thought of his wife's hips, how her pregnant belly had sloped up, the skin stretched so tight it was nearly translucent. The snow at the window glittered in the streetlight and he got up, in just his boxers, the skin on his spindly legs goose pimpled. He stood by the window and watched snow as it fell into the orb of streetlight and then out again into the dark.

THREE

DARK WET MUSH of snow under frozen rain. Everything curtained in purple grayness and ice. Mrs. Chin, a Chinese lady with a wide face and bright lipstick, rented him the new apartment. It was half the price of his studio in the Heights and twice as large, a railroad flat with a kitchen in back, a metal rack for pots, a spice shelf. He opened the cabinet: Zwieback wafers, rice cereal, baby bottles. He'd bought a secondhand high chair and two new terry-cloth bibs.

Down the narrow hall was the living room, where he'd set up his table. The room was gray, but come spring, leaf light would fall over the walls. The adjacent bedroom had a large closet and a small alcove where he'd set up the crib. Decals of rabbits decorated each side. He'd bought organic cotton crib sheets and a bumper pad that would protect the baby's head. He imagined Mary and he curled together on the futon. The scent of her skin like vanilla yogurt. The things she loved, his monk's fringe, his barrel chest, the feminine way he moved his hands, were all things he found humiliating, but she loved them—he kept having to remind himself of that. Mac would argue that he was filled with manic passion. He was, as Mac loved to say, out of spiritual whack. Mac would try to convince him that heaviness was not real presence. But Mac was wrong. A weightless soul was worthless.

John lay on the futon but could not get to sleep. Legs sore from carrying boxes. Back hurting. Heart empty and desolate. He lay there thinking. And thinking some more. Obsessed with the idea that Mary might find her way out to Sunset Park, though she'd never been and had no idea how to find the place. But if only there was a knock on the door and he opened it and she was standing there on the steps. He couldn't take it anymore and got up. Minnows swam at the edge of his eyes, and he realized it was way past midnight and he still hadn't eaten anything.

* * *

Outside the snowflakes were huge and the bodega at the corner was still open. Fluorescent panels lit up a bucket of porktails, plastic packages of cornmeal and ginger biscuits. A sleepy-looking Asian man in a hooded sweatshirt made him a cheese sandwich, and he got a carton of chocolate milk, paid with a ten, sank the change into his pocket and walked back out onto the cold sidewalk.

Stepping off the curb, he looked up the street to his new apartment and imagined Mary, her shoulders, her hair, her body moving in a white nightgown across their living room, and the world was what it was, not a metaphor for something else. John saw its quivering supernatural quality, the electric clarity of its form, its matter, its sharp edges. He saw his palm moving up, disembodied and miraculous.

FOUR

JOHN PUT ON the mask and found his way to the back corner of the hospital room where Mary held the baby. The vaporizer sent out a ribbon of steam and John's shirt stuck to his chest. The baby's face was red and he began to cough, dry and metallic, the sound like the crude devices inside toy dogs. Mary held him high up on her shoulder and patted his back in a firm spiral motion. He shivered along the whole length of his body; his eyeballs stood out and he spit up a stringy line of blood. John grabbed a towel.

The baby lay back on Mary's shoulder, his head resting in the crook of her neck. His breathing was short, his stomach contracting as if choking for breath after a race. The vaporizer kicked on again, sending steam into the room, obscuring Mary's feet and ankles. She pointed to the chairs by the bed. She seemed to want John to say something. Mac always insisted that a period of meditation was crucial before any emotional response. But with Mary premeditation was impossible. Her chest shook and drops of water fell from her eyes and he felt bewildered. The baby lay out on her shoulder like a piece of wet cloth.

"Should we pray?"

Mary tipped her head and closed her eyes; water continued to leak out the sides and made dark spots on the knees of her jeans.

"Dear Father." He sounded stiff and official and he lowered his voice to a whisper. "Be with us here in this place. Let us feel—"

"If anything happens to the baby, I'll kill myself," Mary broke in. "I'm not kidding either. I'm going to steal a surgical knife and slice my wrists." She glanced up at John, her eyes wide and slightly insane.

John felt his face heat up. She was threatening God, not a particularly good strategy, at least judging from the characters in the Old Testament. He tried to touch her hand, but she swung away.

"Visiting hours are over."

"You want me to go?"

Mary nodded and John got his coat. He couldn't feel his head, only a cloudy spot of anxiety that floated between his shoulder blades. Mac would say to breathe deeply, Mac would say to withdraw into prayer, Mac would say he was a fool for getting himself into this situation.

As he walked down the darkened hospital hallway, each room was like a little boat sending out an aura of light. In one room John saw a little boy in pajamas watching television, and in another a mother held a child in a pink sleeper, a drainage tube sticking out the back of the baby's bandaged head.

The hospital's waiting room contained fica plants and plaid couches and smelled of stale coffee and sweat. A Latino man slept on the couch across from John and an older lady in a Miami Beach T-shirt and floral skirt sat with her eyes glued to the television. He thought of the baby's arms draped around Mary's neck and walked to the information desk, the polished wood reflecting the fluorescent light, and he asked the guard if he could call up to the pediatric floor. A nurse answered and said Mary was talking to Dr. Lankwell, but she'd let her know he had decided to wait.

The pressure of the receiver against his ear felt good and he kept it there even after the line went dead; then he walked back and lay down on the couch. He heard the steady stream of cars whooshing past on the BQE, and he was holding a girl's hand. Not Mary but a girl who represented her. Her hand was small and they walked in an apple orchard. There was a teacup resting in tree branches and when she took the cup down, it was filled with blood. Then he was in the monastery basement in the room where the founding monks were buried. A tibia stuck out of the wall and he tried to force the bone back but the tibia broke and a car horn honked; somebody yelled something in Latin, and he was pouring a bottle of Evian over the baby's forehead, darkening and splaying the fine hairs against his small pink scalp. Brother Peter's toothpick crucifix hung on the wall, and he cleared cum off his chest with a Kleenex. Mac grasped his arm and said it's absurd to search for God in terms of preconceived ideas. Mac shook his shoulder until John realized the guard was trying to wake him up.

"The janitor needs to clean," the guard said. He pointed

to a grim-looking man in green driving a metal floor shiner, then motioned to a row of plastic chairs attached to the wall outside the gift shop. "Would you mind moving over to one of them?"

PART IV

MARY

THE BABY SLEPT in the Baby Bjorn while Mary waited in the pediatrician's office. He wore the cotton cap with the ducks on it, and his body slumped to one side of the carrier. She was worried about the kid who coughed as he ran his Tonka truck over the carpet. His mother read the newspaper, and the boy made dry barking sounds without covering his mouth. She watched the receptionist with the complicated braided hairdo and big gold earrings answer the phone and write down a message. The boy coughed so violently that his mother offered a bottle of water from her pocketbook. As the child drank, Mary saw tiny particles, like dust motes in a ray of light, floating around in the liquid.

The nurse walked into the waiting room and called the

baby's name. Mary followed her down the hallway. The walls were papered blue and patterned with tiny rosebuds. She passed the counter with tongue depressors, cotton and gauze in glass canisters and rolls of stickers on wax paper. The eye chart was on one wall and on another, a poster showing all the vegetables that help prevent cancer.

While Mary unsnapped the carrier, laid the sleepy baby on the examination table and took off his terry-cloth jumper, Dr. Lankwell came in and washed her hands at the sink. Mary was a few years younger than the doctor, a short chubby woman with curly hair and a gentle, reassuring manner.

"How's the little fellow?" she asked, pressing her fingers into his stomach below the line of his diaper. His tiny rib cage was delineated and the baby sluggishly opened his eyes. His arms looked pitiful; the pink flesh hung slack on his small bones.

"Still sleepy," Mary said as he turned his tiny anxious face toward her. She stroked his hair and rubbed the palm of his hand.

"How about eating?"

"He nurses some, but his heart is not in it."

The doctor smiled. "That will change, believe me." She

pressed the stethoscope to the baby's chest. His face got red and he began to whine.

"Sounds good," she said, lifting him to a sitting position and supporting his head with her hand loosely around his neck. She placed the stethoscope on his back, her features intent as she moved the disc of metal around on his skin.

"All clear," she finally said. The doctor rotated the baby's arms to make sure his reflexes were good. Her sure hands on the baby's body comforted Mary. The doctor pushed the baby's legs against his stomach gently but firmly with an expertise that made Mary feel her son was a substantial being, not ethereal and ephemeral but resiliently alive.

It wasn't snowing as Mary walked down Henry Street toward the rectory, but it was supposed to snow again tonight. Dusk colored the snow bluish-purple and a bevy of raspberry clouds hung in the sky. The buildings were black, the bare trees were black, the cars moving in the distance were shiny black, all as black and well delineated as a construction paper silhouette against the pink sky. The baby shifted and turned his face up toward hers. *We're not far now, just a couple more blocks.* Mary recited a few lines of *Hop on Pop* and then as much as she could remember of "The Grand Old Duke of York." The baby's eyes widened; he was mesmerized by the shiny button on the collar of her coat.

She walked carefully over the salted sidewalk and mounted the rectory steps. At the top, she dug down into her diaper bag for the house keys. Through the window, she saw Walter seated at the dining room table reading. He had set out blue place mats, white plates and a glass pitcher of water. He'd taken his clerical collar off and rolled the sleeves of his black shirt up to the elbows.

Late in the night Mary heard the garbage truck tip up the recycling Dumpster and the sound of glass bottles shifting against one another. The baby began to cry. She sat up and took him onto her lap. Ever since he got home from the hospital all she wanted to do was look at him. She felt that pinchy tingle signaling her milk coming down, waited for him to open his lips wide and then placed her whole areola into his mouth.

Snowflakes fell into the triangle of street light as the garbage truck retreated and the street grew quiet. Mary knew when she saw the snowflakes, when she heard the sound, as she did now, of snow brushing against glass, that it was a letter from the world of emptiness. She watched the baby's cheek suck in and out. He fell into the rhythm completely and she admired him really, how he knew he deserved to be loved.

ACKNOWLEDGMENTS

Many people have helped me. I am grateful to all of them. Among them are Rick Moody and Susan Wheeler; René Steinke, Natalie Standiford and Elizabeth Mitchell; Madison Bell and Jane Gelfman; Judy Hottensen and Morgan Entrekin; Sister Leslie and Tim Houlihan; my brothers, David and Jonathan Steinke; Miriam Cohen and Rebecca Brown; Douglas Martin and Michael Parker; Rob Sheffield and Marc Bojanowski; Deborah Marks at Dog and Pony Show. I am particularly indebted to Sarah Chalfant and Gillian Blake, and to the work and ideas of Thomas Merton. Many thanks for support to Michael Hudson and my daughter, Abbie Jones Hornburg.

A NOTE ON THE AUTHOR

Darcey Steinke is the author of three previous novels, two of which were *New York Times* Notable Books of the Year. Her novel *Suicide Blonde* has been translated into eight languages. Her short fiction has appeared in the *Literary Review, Story Magazine* and *Bomb*, and her nonfiction has been featured in the *Washington Post*, the *Chicago Tribune*, the *Village Voice, Spin*, and the *New York Times Magazine*. She currently teaches at New School University in New York City and lives with her daughter in Brooklyn.

The text of this book is set in Adobe Caslon, named after the English punch cutter and type founder William Caslon I (1692–1766). Caslon's rather old-fashioned types were modeled on seventeenth-century Dutch designs but found wide acceptance throughout the English-speaking world for much of the eighteenth century until being replaced by newer types toward the end of the century. Used in 1776 to print the Declaration of Independence, they were revived in the nineteenth century and have been popular ever since, particularly among fine printers. There are several digital versions, of which Carol Twombly's Adobe Caslon is one.

DATE DUE
